Mr Scruff

SIMON JAMES

WALKER BOOKS
AND SUBSIDIARIES
LONDON • BOSTON • SYDNEY • AUCKLAND

First published 2019 by Walker Books Ltd
87 Vauxhall Walk, London SE11 5HJ
This edition published 2020

2 4 6 8 10 9 7 5 3 1

This book has been typeset in Minion
Printed in China

British Library Cataloguing in Publication Data: a catalogue record
for this book is available from the British Library

ISBN 978-1-4063-9291-3

www.walker.co.uk
www.simonjamesbooks.com

This is Polly

she belongs to Molly.

This is Eric

he belongs to Derek.

This is Martha

she belongs to Arthur.

But who's this?

It's Mr Scruff...

For Mr Scruff there's no one.

This is Mick

he belongs to Rick.

And this is Lawrence

he belongs to Florence.

But things are looking rough,
for poor old Mr Scruff.

Wait a minute! Who's this...?

It's Jim!

They seem to like each other.

"But Jim," says Dad,
"are you sure?
He's so BIG
and you're so small!
I can't see it working.
No, not at all!"

"He's so OLD," says Mum,
"and you're so young.
Surely a puppy would
be more fun?"

"No," says Jim.
"He needs a home.
A place to call his very own.
That's what he needs.
And that's enough
for me –
and Mr Scruff."

So, while
Polly has Molly,
Eric has Derek,
Martha has Arthur,
Mick has Rick,
Lawrence has Florence,
now …
Mr Scruff belongs to Jim!

And though it doesn't rhyme,
it's all worked out just fine.

But, wait a minute. Who's this...?

It's Mr Gruff.
He's come to choose a dog.

Here's a little pup.
They seem to like each other...

"I'm so BIG,
and you're so small.
But that doesn't matter.
No, not at all!"

Mr Gruff is happy.
It's the perfect
dog for him.

Can you guess the puppy's name?
Well, of course –

it's Tim!

The End

Simon James

Simon James is an award-winning author and illustrator of books for children – creator of the much-loved character Baby Brains and of touching tales exploring a child's unique relationship with nature.

978-1-4063-8315-7

978-1-4063-6740-9

978-1-4063-6053-0

978-1-84428-522-8

978-1-4063-5251-1

978-1-4063-3842-3

978-1-84428-467-2

978-1-4063-0849-5

978-1-4063-0846-4

978-1-4063-0845-7

Available from all good booksellers

www.walker.co.uk